I Saw You Planting Roses

Jordan McCrary

I would like thank my family, the sisters of the Sigma Omega Omega chapter of Alpha Kappa Alpha Sorority Inc. and my literature teacher, Almena Mayes for supporting me throughout this creative process.

Ms. Mechelle,

Thank you for your support!♡

"Plant roses."

Jordan Murray

The Prologue

When you are a child, your parents make most of the choices for you. They typically know what is best for you and generally want the best for you. Well, this is what happened to our family. When I was in elementary school, my mom identified a school that she thought would be great for me and my brother. This meant disrupting our current situation. We were in a school that we liked, around kids we were familiar with and had our routine. What we learned is that the new school situation would not only change who we saw in school, but would require us to pack up and physically move to a new community.

My neighborhood was the only one I had ever known. The only thoughts that ran through my mind were, *I had figured out all of the nooks and hiding places. We have beautiful roses in the yard that bloom a vibrant red. I am familiar with getting around our house and I am not sure I want to go to a new school or community. Do I get any say so in this?*

My mom had already started looking for a new place for us to move into. She wanted to get our house ready to be rented or sold. Sold? Wait a minute. Does this mean we are never coming back? We may need to think about this! The mall is not far, there are cool places to eat and I like it out here! My friends are here! I like the neighbors! I did not have anything to compare it to but I knew I liked it.

What will this new school offer, I wondered. Will the kids be friendly? Why do we have to wear uniforms? I wasn't really interested in this at all. My brother, on the other hand, seemed to be open to something new. He wasn't really attached to his school so he was ready to go. He acted like it was a new adventure or something. He had to wear a uniform at his other school so I guess he was ok with wearing the same clothes every day. My mom likes the uniform option so that she does not have to think about what clothes we need to wear. *What about what I want? I want to stay at my school, in my neighborhood and with my friends!*

We had been driving around for months looking for a new place. Some of the places were okay but it was still not our house. We had to look for a house in the specific school zone. We had seen several great houses but they were not in the school zone we needed. This was a lot of trouble to go through just for a school.

We came across a few nice houses. I could see myself in a couple of them. Some of the neighborhoods were nice and pretty. I started to think that the move might not be that bad after all. My mom told me to be open to new things.

We pulled into the yard of a house that we had visited before. This time, however, the real estate agent was not here. My dad said welcome to your new home. My first thought was…*where are the kids? I hope the neighbors are nice.*

That lady was in the yard planting rose bushes the last time we were here…

Chapter 1 - The Move

We spent 10 years in the old house. It was home. I knew all the spaces, I knew all the nooks and crannies, I knew all the noises and I loved it. We were close to the grocery store. We were close to the mall, but we were not close to my parents' jobs. This was hard for my parents. They always complained about the traffic, the long drive, and being tired when they got home.

My mom got a new job and it was in a great area. She loved her new job but it was a little further out and I think I mentioned she hated the drive. Near her office was this great school and it was in a pretty good community. Once my mom decided she wanted us at that school, I knew we had to move. She would come home talking about the school, the area, and all the great things my brother and I could get involved with. All I could think about was having to leave my friends. In the old neighborhood, we had lots of friends all up and down the street. We moved to the neighborhood when it was brand new. Many of the neighbors were new parents and all of the kids grew up together. We had the largest yard so, over the years, everyone would come to play at our house. Mostly, we played kickball. My mom would bring out snacks and then all kids would disburse to their houses for homework, dinner, or to just to go home. If I'm being completely honest, everyone had to go inside when the street lights came on. It was nice. The moms and dads knew each other and the kids could go to the neighbors' houses and have fun.

We all rode the school bus and when my parents couldn't get to the house after school, my grandma would be waiting. My grandma was recently retired and still wanted to go out and about. She would drive to the house and wait patiently for us. Then, she would take us in the house thinking we needed a break. We, however, always wanted to run outside with our friends.

Grandma would start cooking dinner; which was perfect because we would always come in the house dirty and hungry. We were happy.

So the search began. Each weekend, we would go to explore new neighborhoods that would get us closer to my parents' jobs and zoned for the school my mom wanted us to attend. It looked like just a school to me. As a matter of fact, my school looked better than this school.

"Where are the buses?", I asked. My mom said that there were no buses and that we would have to either walk to school or get dropped off by our parents. *Hmmm... Not sure about this school. What is a charter school anyway?*

Red, pink, and white are all the colors I see as we drive into our new neighborhood. I wonder if there are new kids I will get to meet or if I will even like our new house. I notice one house next door that is completely fenced in. I think nothing of it at the time. I just keep looking out the window. All the houses are nice. The green lawns are lush and adorned with roses and other flowers in all different colors but I can't help but wonder, *what about the houses that don't have any flowers or roses? Does that mean there is no love, there's no loss, there's no anything*? These are the random thoughts I have looking out of the window as we drive into our new neighborhood.

"This is it." my dad says as we drive up to a massive beige mansion. "This is our new house? It's huge for just four people," "No silly, those are our new neighbors. This is ours." My mother tells me as she points to a smaller, but still large, grey house with a stone mailbox. We get out of the car and to the left we see a couple driving into the house next door. The woman, looking upset, gets out the car and slams the door. I don't pay much attention to it though.

Good Morning," I said as coincidentally we are both at our mailboxes at seven in the morning. *I wonder what she's doing up this early? It looks like she was wiping dirt off her clothes.* "Sierra, I noticed you were looking at me through that window of yours last night," she says walking up to me. At this point, she was close enough to reach out and grab me. There was a long pause…and we just stared at each other. "What all did you see last night?" she questions as she seems to stare into my soul. I think she knows I saw her planting roses.

My brother and I try to get situated and he decides to explore the neighborhood on his bike. Our new house is in a cul-de-sac and there doesn't seem to be a lot of traffic.

My mom is in the yard assessing the flower beds to see what we need to make the front yard look nice. Meanwhile, I pulled out a lawn chair from the U-Haul truck, sat in the yard and began to read my book. At our old house, we had a variety of flowers in the yard so I am sure my mom will plant new ones to make this house feel like home. While she is standing in the yard, a lady comes from behind the fence next door. She's the neighbor in the fenced off yard. She walks toward my mom and appears to introduce herself and chat. My brother and I look on from afar as my mom waves for us to come over.

"Kids, this is Ms. Rose, she lives next door. She came out because she heard kids' voices in the neighborhood."

I inspected Ms. Rose as she stuck out her hand to shake ours. She looked like she was around the age of my grandmother.

"Hi Ms. Rose" said my brother. Then he took off on his bike. After politely greeting our new neighbor, I went back to my chair to read my book. My mom told us later that she had said that very few children lived in the neighborhood and that she was glad to hear us. Soon, other neighbors would stop by to say hello and welcome us to the neighborhood.

It was starting to get dark outside so I knew the street lights would come on soon. I hadn't even realized that my mom and brother had gone inside already. I had been too into my amazing book. It was about this girl who had fallen in love with a boy she was tutoring. I know it's cliché but those types of stories just do something to me.

When all the little details are there, I feel as if I'm actually in the book. I enjoy reading and since Ms. Rose said there were not a lot of children in the neighborhood, expect I may be reading a lot of books.

My mom does not let us stay inside to just watch television. She always makes us go outside to get fresh air. There is a nice patio so maybe that will become my new favorite place in the new house. I enjoy reading all types of books but I truly enjoy mysteries. Sometimes the culprit is who you least expect and I enjoy all the twists and turns in mystery books.

As I walk inside, I see my parents unpacking boxes in the kitchen. It doesn't even feel real. I make my way up the front stairs and see my brother putting all his stuff in the room down the hall. *I guess he already claimed his territory.* There were four bedrooms upstairs. I know my parents have the master so I went to the empty room towards the back of the house. I opened the door and see that the people who lived here before obviously had a daughter in this room. It had rose pink walls with stars on the walls and ceiling. I noticed a large window in the corner that had a view of our front yard and our neighbors' backyard. I have the perfect idea for this cute little corner. I could make it into a nook area where I could read away.

As the weeks go by we get settled into the house. The boxes start to make their exit and it's starting to feel more like home. I finish putting all of my clothes inside my dresser and closet. It feels good not to have all those boxes just lying around everywhere.

Once I finish, I plop down on my bed and just stare at the ceiling fan spinning. We have been in this house for almost a month, but I can't help but continue to wonder about the family that lived here before us. I wonder what they were like. *Where did the go?*

As I was in deep thought, my mother barged into my room. "Sierra, make sure you get enough sleep tonight, we have the open house for school tomorrow morning." With that, she just shuts the door and vanishes.

Ugh… school! Don't get me wrong, I absolutely love learning, but the whole idea of being the new kid at school didn't really sit well with me. I didn't want to prepare to stand up and share about my summer or where I'm from. It's not like I moved from another country. All we did was move across the city to be closer to my dads' workplace and go to this new school. I guess I'm going to have to face those weird conversations and awkward silences at some point. So, why not do it on my first day of high school? Great!

The next day my brother and I had to wake up early so we could go to the open house to get everything sorted out so we could start school soon. Our new school was across town so we had lots of time for my mom to chat with us in the car. We were trapped and she knows she can have our undivided attention. She asks us about our feelings, what's going on in our lives, if we have talked to our old friends. Her topics include anything she can discuss in about twenty minutes. Sometimes we feel chatty, sometimes we want to take a nap.

At my old school, I honestly dreaded going to open house at the beginning of each school year. I had many friend at my old school.

I had two special friends that I did everything with, Zoe and Grayson. I miss them a lot. We always talked about going through high school together. *It was going to be us against the world.* Sadly, I had to move to this new side of town filled with people I don't know. My brother pulled me out of my deep thoughts with a punch to my shoulder. "Mom said to hurry up and get out of the car." I rolled my eyes as I get out of the car. *My brother really gets on my nerves*.

My brother is too cooperative. He didn't have any problems with going to a new school. He says change is good and he will make new friends. Blah. Blah. He was just fine with all of this. I, however, miss my old school and all of my old friends. I didn't want to change. Although change is good, I don't like it.

The first day of school… I don't want to seem like those cliché teen movies, where the person is excited about their first day of high school. So, I won't. I don't think there is anything here that I'm looking forward to; except maybe lunch, and going home. Actually, I am excited about my advanced computer science class. I've always enjoyed computers and the counselors told me I would be one of only two freshmen in that class, *which is pretty cool. I guess those summer programs paid off!*

As we pull up to the front of the building, my mom is trying to park so she can take pictures. She does every year. First day of school pictures. I tried to hurry out of the car so she didn't even have a chance to pull the car around the parking lot. I heard her yelling as we got out the car. There were parents everywhere taking pictures of the first day of school. It looks like there are lots of new kids at the school. They look awkward and nervous… like me. You can also tell the kids that had gone there for middle school. They seemed to greet each other with familiarity and the parents seemed to know each other. They posed for their pictures; some even had signs with their grade on them. The school has a middle school and a high school; so there are kids everywhere.

The school is much larger than I thought. Like way larger. It's huge! While I walked in with my brother, there were kids way younger than us running into the building.

After observing all the teachers and administrators, I learned that half of the building was a middle school and the other half belonged to the high school.

As the day went by I felt like I was growing accustomed to the 'norms' of the school. There was a presentation after our first period class where the principal gathered all the students into the auditorium.

I know for a fact that my old school didn't have an auditorium. Every time we would have an assembly or any event, it was in the cafeteria. The cafeteria had a small stage in the front.

Our principal, Mr. McMichael, was introducing us to the new grade level teachers and welcoming us into the high school. After the introduction, the ninth and tenth graders went to lunch. I didn't know anyone at the school, so I had to sit wherever I could. Across from me were some girls who were hugging each other and screaming. Loud is an understatement in this situation. I'm assuming they had not seen each other over summer break. I just minded my business though.

I decided to eat my lunch while catching up on my Netflix shows. As I was enjoying my leftovers from yesterday, I felt someone sit in the chair next to me. I looked over and I saw a boy sitting next to me. He was acting as if he knew me. As I continued to eat my food, he started saying things. I turned towards him and he said,

"Hi, let me introduce myself. Jace, Jace Elliot."

I examined him for a quick second before responding. He was a charming boy, cute, with a little bit of edge. He could potentially be my first friend at this school.

"Sierra, Sierra Nottingham." I stuck out my hand to shake his.

He ended up telling me more about student created 'norms'. Basically the social status and rules of each group and grade. He eventually went back to his seat after asking questions about me and where I was from.

Over the course of the day, Jace would stop me in the halls to 'check on me' or just to say hey and bye. By the end of the day I had started to grow accustomed to the huge building where I'd be spending the next few years.

Surprisingly, I think that the thing I liked most about this school is the uniforms. I know right, sue me. It's just easy not to waste time figuring out what I plan to wear.

One day at my old school, I was so frustrated with my wardrobe, I didn't realize I missed the bus. Sometimes I even planned my outfits out the weekend before. I obviously couldn't wear the same thing each week, so I had to plan strategically. Wearing the same thing every day really helps. Plus, you can look cute and snazzy in a uniform.

It was finally the end of the day and the lady who sits at the front desk was making the daily announcements. She was talking about a school event at the beginning of the school year called 'Late Night Lock-In'. I wasn't always into the social events at school, but I thought to myself, *it's a new year, and a new me. Maybe I should just suck it up and go. Maybe it will be fun.* It seemed like most of the students planned to attend. This was supposed to be a way to meet new people, meet the staff and actually learn more about the school. As usual my brother is all in and ready to go. There were a few people that looked familiar. My brother said he remembered a few people from some of the summer camps we attended and from the youth center we went to periodically. *I have to stay positive and open minded. First impressions are lasting ones.*

Chapter 2 - The Window

It's quite an adventure looking out of the window in my room. At our old house, all I could see was our backyard. I missed all the action, unless I was in my mom's room. From mom's window I could see the kids in the neighborhood gathering and would immediately yell, "Mom can we go outside?"

"Yes, but stay out of my roses", my mom would respond.

I miss our old neighborhood. We had kids to play with after school. Plus, all of the kids in our neighborhood knew each other from school so we were even closer. That was cool. Have I mentioned… we haven't seen any kids in the new neighborhood? To be completely honest I haven't seen a lot of people in general, not just kids. *Weird.* The few times that I have seen people in the neighborhood, they are usually working in their yard or something. Then, there is that speed walker with the big stick... *I wonder where the dogs are around here*. All I have seen are deer roaming around looking at us like they are thinking, "What are y'all doing in my yard?"

In the new house, my room is on the front side of the house and I have a large window and where I get the see everything. All of the walkers, all of the cars that have gotten lost that need to turn around, all of the garbage trucks, the neighbor across the street that is always doing something in his yard. *Why is everyone always working in their yard*?

As we roamed around the neighborhood, we saw a yard with a Yard of the Month sign posted front and center. Now I get it. Obviously, everyone wants that small little sign in their front yard so everyone knows how much effort they put into their yards.

The community has a "Yard of the Month" program and neighbors are selected each month by the landscape committee. The winners get a yard sign in their yard.

The people whose yards are always nice are retired so I guess they have extra time on their hands to make their yards look gorgeous. Maybe one day we will have the sign. Then again maybe not. We have very busy lives. Outside of school, my brother and I play sports. So, we really aren't home a lot. I really think that soon my mom will start paying someone to maintain our yard.

To me, the sign seems pointless for us because we live in the very back of the neighborhood. No one even comes back here except the police who patrol the neighborhood.

Looking out of the window, I see my dad pull into the driveway and as he walks to get the mail, a gentleman comes from Ms. Rose's yard and they start to talk. My dad shook his hand and started pointing. *I wonder what they are talking about.* They laugh a little and the man returns to the fenced in yard. *I wonder why they have a fence around the entire yard. They are the only house on the street with a full yard fence.*

It's almost like the Twilight Zone. We have been here a few months and we should have seen a few kids by now. Everyone seems older and perhaps there should be grandkids running around. On our way to school, we see a school bus stop on the main road so there have to be kids somewhere. My mom says kids are different now. She says that they stay in the house, play video games and don't appreciate being outside. She still makes us go outside! I guess that's when she has her "Me Time."

I enjoy being outside. I just don't have anyone else to hang out with other than my brother. He's cool and all but we need to find some kids around here.

We walked through the neighborhood and found the clubhouse. It had a playground and a pool. It looked like there may be different phases to the neighborhood.

Perhaps we are where older neighbors live and maybe the kids are in the new area. In the mornings, I figured we would see a few kids waiting on their bus or even in the cars driving out but so far… nothing. No kids. We will have to pop out at different times. Our school starts early and we end late so perhaps we miss the action in the neighborhood. *I really hope that is what it is.*

Chapter 3 - The Bishop

The man that dad was talking to was Ms. Roses' husband. Turns out he is the leader of a local church and likes to play golf. That's probably what he was talking to my dad about.

When we are outside, he waves and we wave back. He seems nice enough. The gates open and a car pulls out of the yard and it's the Bishop. He stops to talk to my mom who is still trying to get the yard together in the front. They seem to exchange a laugh and he drives away. She resumes planting purple flowers around the mailbox. I don't see the Bishop that often, but he periodically walks around the yard on the phone, gets in the car, and then drives away. He always waves hello and seems like a nice man.

Periodically there are lots of cars up and down the street near the Bishop's house. My mom said a famous rapper used to live there. *Perhaps that's why it's all fenced in.* What are they doing over there and they better not block our driveway this time. *Famous is relative.*

My mom is always talking about back in the day. I've never heard of the rapper she says used to live in the Bishop's house. My mom tries to play his music but it has a lot of cursing so I can't really get a feel for the music. *I wonder if the rapper used to* throw big parties and go wild in the house. I hope the Bishop prayed over the property just in case.

I see the Bishop now, driving to the gate and waiting patiently for it open. Luckily, I can see his whole driveway, and pretty much his whole house from my window. He drives in slowly. He gets out of his car and looks around as if someone was following him. *Hmm. Maybe someone is after him and I need to stay alert.* That's my civic duty, right?

What is a Bishop? We call the leader of our church “Father”. *I will have to look this up and see what it means*. I rummage through my backpack for my computer. The Bishop is a senior member of the Christian clergy; typically, in charge of a diocese and empowered to confer holy orders. What? That didn’t really help me. I just know he is in charge at his church. He’s looking this way. How did he see me from my window, though? I just wave, turn and go about my business.
I still don’t see any kids.

Over time I have learned the schedules of most of the neighbors. The man across the street seems to travel a lot. People are always jumping out of their cars to take pictures at his house. The neighbor next to him have gaudy decorations in their yard with several ornamental balls, rock art, and they project different images on their house based on the season. Many animals roam around the neighborhood, especially deer.

I can always tell when the Bishop's gate opens because it rattles the ground. I have gotten used to it but I am still aware. At night the lights shine into my window so I know I have to keep the blinds closed if I want to get some rest. There are lots of cars coming and going next door. *I wonder what's going on?* Maybe they offer prayer or bible study at the house.

Chapter 4 - School

I've been at my new school for a couple weeks now and I just have to say, this school is something else. There are all types of kids. But I actually like it here because everyone is cool with everyone.

There is no tension between grades or even other students. I feel as if I've adjusted very well. Jace and I have gotten very close, closer than I thought I would get with anyone here. My last close friends were Zoe and Grayson. I had been friends with them since we were in diapers. Those two are the only people outside of my family that I trust. That was until now; Jace is such a good person to be around. Nothing is forced when I'm around him. He has even introduced me to some of his friends; Jass and Dallas.

Jass is actually his twin sister, which is pretty cool. But, I like hanging with Jace when it's just us. He's like the brother I've always wanted. I know I have an older brother and he is cool but this is different.

Jace actually listens and responds without getting smart. Not sure if I like him, like him, but he is cool and is making the adjustment to the new school easier.

My classes and teachers are okay, but I imagine everyone puts their best foot forward at the beginning of the school year. I am still trying to figure people out and see where people are from. In a charter school, people come from all over the city, not just from the community like a zoned school It is interesting the see how the kids interact and you can tell the kids who were here in middle school. They already know a lot about the school, things to get involved in and already know lots of kids. I will have to explore the website and see what types of things I can get involved with at school. The high school is relatively new. They have only had a couple of graduating classes. I am sure my mom will be asking what kind of clubs I signed up for.

I think I plan to just lay low and see how things operate around here.

The school culture is a little different. Everyone looks the same with the uniform so no one really stands out. The school leaders stand at the door making sure you are in full uniform and you get pulled to the side if you are out of compliance. It seems like they would let the students have some way to express themselves.

One of the other students shared that the uniforms have more options than they have had in the past. He said they allow "dress down days" or causes or you can donate a dollar and dress down. We will see how it all works out. *I hope I do not outgrow my regular clothes.* It has been much easier getting dressed in the morning. I do not have to think about what to wear, how it will look, or anything; just put on the uniform and go. I guess that's not bad. We will have to see…

Chapter 5 - The Kids Are Somewhere

We have gotten comfortable in the house and have our daily routine. We don't see any kids on our street but we see people in the morning traffic. Little heads poke out and periodically we will see a teen walking towards the bus stop. We don't attend the community school but I imagine if we did, we would have met kids that live in the neighborhood. I see several stickers for a variety of charter schools and private schools, so I guess kids are all over the city.

One day, while we were at the community pool, my mom stopped to meet a neighbor. The neighbor said she had a teen daughter and that they should get the children together. I had never actually seen a child, but there were kids at the pool this time. Little kids. Kids that wanted to splash around in the water. Kids that still use floaties to swim. So my mom goes over to meet the parents and they break out into a hug. My mom knows everyone. Everywhere she goes she knows someone. There is nowhere that we can go and it doesn't turn into a 30-minute conversation with an old co-worker or classmate So we meet the friend and her kids. I am looking for other teens to connect with. Where are the kids or should I say teens because this kid just splashed me with water…?

My mom went to high school in this area so it was like moving back home for her. She always talks about kids from her neighborhood and how much fun it was growing up in this area. She always goes on and on about how the community has changed and kids and young families moved out of the city. I wish I could experience some of the things my mom describes. It seems like she had a great time. She always says I have to create my experiences, get involved and have fun. She says it doesn't just happen. Students have to make suggestions, support their sports teams, and get involved with things at the school. I guess. There is not a football team so she says we have to create traditions. That's easy for her to say when she went to a school with all kinds of traditions and she still goes back to her school for things now, including football games.

Wait, who is that person Ms. Rose is talking to in the dark? That doesn't look like the Bishop's car. She looks like she's up to something. I can't quite put my finger on it but something isn't right with Ms. Rose. I just get questionable vibes from her.

Chapter 6 - Where is Bishop?

So it's been a few days since I've seen Bishop. Now that I am familiar with him and some of the other neighbors I know their patterns. Since I have this big window, I might as well help keep the neighborhood safe. *Maybe he is traveling or something.*

A few more days go by and still no Bishop. *Where is Bishop?* While she was in the yard, I asked my mom, who seems friendly with Ms. Rose, if she had seen Bishop lately. She shrugged her shoulders and said "No, I haven't seen him or noticed anything. Maybe he is traveling or doing a revival." *Hmmm maybe.*

A few more days go by and I still haven't seen the Bishop or his car. I'm not nosey, I just pay attention. I ask my mom again because Ms. Rose seems to acting a little standoffish over there. She hasn't been coming over to our yard while we are outside, which isn't like her. Usually she just tends to the existing flowers, but lately she has pulled out shovels and seems to be digging over there. *She's an older lady and may hurt something with all that digging.* That sure is a long deep hole for a few rose bushes, I tell my mom. My mom gives me the side eye and pulls out of the driveway. We wave.

As we drive out of the subdivision, I tell my mom that I think Ms. Rose has been acting a little sketchy lately. Sketchier than usual. And, I tell her, I haven't seen the Bishop lately. My mom explains that he could be traveling, he could be sick in the hospital…anything. I'm sure we would have gotten a message from the Homeowners Association if something bad had happened. What mom doesn't know is that I see what goes on in the neighborhood, and I have a full view of their house. So I see things…

Mom still can't quite get the yard the way she wants so she has had to call in a landscaping company. Our house had been empty for a while before we bought it and so the yard needed lots of work. Even though my mom has been working hard in the yard, it still needs help. Grateful for his arrival, the landscaper gets a big hug. Like I said, *my mom seems to know everyone*. He went to high school and college with her and he used to live in "the old neighborhood."

Ms. Rose was in her yard looking... watching us from her garage…just standing there. When the landscaper leaves, I tell mom again, Ms. Rose is up to something. Where is the Bishop? We both look over to the neighbor's yard. "Hi Ms. Rose."

Reading mystery novels probably makes my imagination more vivid. *Am I over think this situation with the Bishop.* No! I am being a concerned neighbor. I haven't seen him or his car. If he is doing a revival or something, it seems like he would come home, refresh his clothes and check on his wife. *Did he leave her*? So many questions. What I do know is that the Bishop is missing and Mrs. Rose is acting strange.

Chapter 7 - Rose Bushes

I am actually worried about the Bishop. It has been at least a month and still there has been no sign of him. My mom has taken note of this as well. Not as much as me, but she's starting to notice it. She is still trying to convince me that everything over there is fine, but I'm not going to ignore my gut feeling.

What my mom doesn't know is that for the past couple weeks since the Bishop mysteriously disappeared, I've been writing in one of the many journals I received as birthday presents.

I try to take notes on mostly everything in the neighborhood. I have notes on peoples' cars, notes on the dog walkers of the neighborhood, and especially the rare occasions I see children. Sometimes I even make up names for people I see since I know very few people.

Don't call me paranoid. I have notes on all the days and nights that I happen to see Ms. Rose doing "*work*" in her backyard.

One time, my mom had to work late and we had to take an Uber home from school. I just so happened to look over to Ms. Roses' driveway to see a delivery of wooden planks. At first, I thought she was building a flower bed for her new flowers. However, there were multiple sizes and lengths of the wood, so it had to have been a more intricate project. I was unlocking the door to go inside when I glanced back over to their yard. There she was again…just standing there…watching us. I could see her silhouette in their upstairs window. It was almost as if she was watching us since we got out the car. Depending on how long she had been standing there, I know she saw me looking into her yard and at her deliveries. I felt like my heart stopped as I ran into my house. I remember that night so vividly. I remember it even more because I made sure I wrote down everything that I saw.

We went outside and found that Ms. Rose had the shovel and was digging more holes. *Now why on earth would that woman be digging holes in her yard this late at night? It's almost 10 o'clock at night.* This time near that back fence. "Mom, I think Ms. Rose killed her husband." I said. My mom looked at me and said that I had gone too far with this. Unless she can give me a better explanation, I'm going with this!

Chapter 8 - Just like a Crime Show

My mom is the biggest fan of Forensic Files and Snapped so she knows exactly what I am suggesting. *I believe that Ms. Rose has killed the Bishop and buried him under the rose bushes.* What else would she need all of that wood and that huge hole in the back for? She seems like a nice old lady. "*If he isn't under the bushes where is he*?" I asked. Now, everyone is on the lookout for the Bishop.

My aunt came over for a visit and my mom shared what was going on. My aunt jumped right in with her own theories. Mom yelled, "Jan, don't buy into this! The Bishop is probably out praying for people."

Aunt Jan and I looked at each other and whispered, "He's under the bushes." She nods her head in agreement.

Once my mom leaves, I walk over to the living room window where you can see the neighbors' backyard. Ms. Rose was back there working…again. "God knows what she's working on,".

Me and my aunt went outside and stood in the driveway periodically glancing over at Ms. Rose's yard. The next thing we knew, Ms. Rose walked over to us. *I wonder what she wants.* "Brace yourself Aunt Jan. We don't know what she is capable of right now", I cautiously say.

"You have done such a great job with your yard. Your rose bushes grew in nicely." says Ms. Rose. I don't think she knew she was talking to my aunt. My mom and my aunt basically look like twins. I stood off to the side because I was not so sure what Ms. Rose might do.

My aunt continued with the small talk while I just watched and monitored her from afar just in case she tried to pull something. I think she was just trying to get a sense of what we know and what we have seen in her rose garden. She eventually heads back to her fenced yard but not before waving at me, my aunt and my brother; who had made his way outside. We all give a smile and wave back. She goes in the garage and brings out the shovel. Alarmed, we all run back into the house and up to my room to look out the window. *What is she up to today*?

Everyone else goes about their day and I monitor the window. As I walk by and glance out the window, Ms. Rose looks back. *She knows I am watching*. Feeling nervous I head downstairs with the others.

What have I gotten myself into? What do we really know about the neighbors? What church is the Bishop really affiliated with? What started out as a small joke, has blossomed and we still haven't seen the Bishop.

I asked my mom what she really knew about the neighbors. Did we do any research on this neighborhood? It's still weird that we don't see kids around here. We just see a few cars coming and going on our street. Although it is a nice, quiet neighborhood, I think something strange is happening and I can't quite put my finger on it.

I asked my mom for the homeowners' book that gives a little history of the community and I think I will do a little research. As I go to my room and glance out the window, I see a hole in the fence next door by the woods. I don't remember that hole in the fence. As I look across the yard, I see a fresh pile of dirt and Ms. Rose's shovel.

Oh my God. She moved the body.

Chapter 9 - Redirecting my Attention

Now that I am more involved in school, I have had to redirect my attention to other things. I am playing a few sports and learning to do my hair in new styles, and exploring makeup.

My window gives the perfect lighting and I get to keep up with what is happening on our street. One of the local politicians lives on our street and is always in the news and the police have been driving up and down the street lately. I wonder if they are here for the politician or if they are also looking for the Bishop. Probably the first thing though. I'm sure I'm the only one who has noticed his absence.

The politician stays in the news so we never know what may happen on any given day. What I do know is that it is August and he still has his holiday lights up and turns them on periodically. It burns my mom up! She says it's fine to keep the lights in the bushes if you are too lazy to take them down each year but why turn on the holiday lights mid-year? Can we have Labor Day, Halloween and Thanksgiving?

I am looking forward to another school year and hope that perhaps we will get a few new student transfers. Everything at school seems so routine now and we need a little excitement. Because we do not have a football team, I go to my mom's high school football games and watch how she chats with all of her old friends. It's like they are still in high school. But at least the band is pretty good. Some of these kids look familiar. Actually I know that kid. He use to go my school. I wonder what made them transfer.

After an exciting game we watch the band march out. The spirit is electric when they win the game. People are gathered in the parking lot happy and laughing. I really enjoy going to other school's football games since the sports at my school haven't started up yet. All of my school's homecoming activities happen during basketball season.

We make our way through the traffic and head home. As we drive up the hill, we can see the reflection of blue and red lights. There appears to be an officer stopping traffic. We live on a dead end street so this is our only way home. So of course I immediately think that the police found out Ms. Rose has the Bishop under the bushes or something. Or maybe they finally found some kids. I can't really see and the neighbors are starting to gather. I wonder what's going on as some cars start to turn around. My mom waits patiently for the officer to come to her window and she explains that we live on the street. She produces her license and asks if we can go to our house. I have to use the restroom so I have my fingers crossed. The officer goes to talk to another officer and they seem to be trying to figure out what to do. I see people standing around shaking their head so clearly the neighbors see something. It was only a few minutes but in my mind it seemed like forever. The officer waived us through. Finally! Thank you! Now let me see what's going on down here. Welp, It's not Ms. Rose.

There were police cars all along the street, I looked back and a local news truck was coming in behind us. Now I'm scared. What's going on around here? It appears to be at the politician's house. I look at my brother as he looks up and says… "Got him."

There are things happening on both ends of the street. When I said I was redirecting my attention, I didn't mean to another situation on my street. In 3...2...1…

Here goes my mom speculating on what has been going on with the politician and why he needs to take those Christmas lights down.

I guess my mom may have been right. I was so focused on Ms. Rose and those bushes that I have been missing the action on the other side of the street. So here is what my mom thinks she knows. A few years ago, the politician neighbor…. let's call him Bernard. Bernard is a good name. According to mom, Bernard got his girlfriend pregnant and he had to marry her because it wouldn't look good to not be married and having a baby as he aspired to be in a higher office. So word on the street is that he didn't really want to marry her but she is from a prominent Atlanta family and they wouldn't have it any other way. Plus, he needed to appear to be a family man. I don't see the big deal but okay. So Bernard has been elected to his next office and word around the neighborhood is that he still dates someone else and the marriage is a sham. But the bigger news is that he has abused his power and may be indicted on several charges. So while I've been on the lookout for the bushes in Ms. Rose's yard, I should have been monitoring Bernard. My mom is casually going to the mailbox. She never gets the mail but today she wants to get the mail and sprays the bushes and just linger outside.

The officers appear to be taking things from the house in brown bags. My brother says they are evidence bags. They are probably raiding his house looking for evidence. I hope that baby is not there. Whatever it is, I don't think the baby should see this. I wonder what he did. Let my mom tell it, it's the Christmas lights because she thinks that a major violation, just straight up illegal. But I think it is more serious. We will have to watch the news and see what really happened. Here comes Ms. Rose from inside her gated yard, stopping to get my mom's attention and see what's happening. My mom is shaking her head and pointing. Ms. Rose should be glad they are not at her house this time. She waves because she knows I'm watching. Thinking to myself… I know what you're up to. You've been spared this time Ms. Rose. You have been spared.

The next morning, we turn on the news and sure enough, Bernard has been accused of several things, his house was raided and of course he claims that he is an innocent man and he has done nothing wrong and is looking forward to defending his name in court. Good Luck Bernard

Chapter 10 - She Looks familiar

There is a lady we periodically see at the school. I am sure she is a parent. Every time my mom sees her she says, “That lady looks so familiar.” We can’t put our finger on it, but my mom knows people from everywhere. It’s unusual that my mom doesn't approach her because if people look familiar, she usually walks up to them, then tries to figure out if she knows them or not. As we are leaving school, the lady’s car is in front of us. We appear to be going in the same direction, we take the same exit, then turn into the same subdivision. So maybe we have seen her at a community event. But no, my mom thinks it’s something else.

As we go about our lives, she appears more frequently. Here we go, I think to myself as my mom gets out of the car to approach the lady. I know every word she is about to say.

“Hi, I have been seeing you around the school. Where do I know you from?” The lady smiles and they try to figure it out. When my mom puts her hand on her hip… She has figured it out. They laugh and my mom starts pointing. The lady looks our way and now she is headed to the car. Geesh. Here we go…

Now that I see her, she does look familiar. She comes to the car and speaks to me and my brother. She is familiar but I can’t place a finger on it. We smile and speak. They walk back to her car and I assume she is waiting on her child. Out walks Derek and he gets into the car. But only after my mom has looked him over and he shakes her hand. Derek is one of Jace’s teammates from the soccer team. He is in my Computer Science class. The Moms chat for a few more moments and we take off behind them both headed home. My mom gets back in the car and says “Do you all remember her? That is Coach Jerry's wife." My brother says "Our old soccer coach? That was 8 years ago. I don't know how we would've remembered the coach let alone his wife."

Apparently she lives in our neighborhood and when my mom told her where we lived she said to be careful. What does that mean? Bernard or Ms. Rose? Now I have to watch my back. I will definitely have to talk to Derek to see what his mom means by be careful.

Now I know that if ever need a ride at least one person is in the neighborhood and we can carpool. When we were driving down the street I saw another student from our school. My mom asked by I did not wave and say hello. She asked if he needed a ride.

"I do not know, Mom but you're a stranger," I told her. I don't really know him; he just goes to the school. I am not sure students today are as friendly as they may have been back in her day. I image as I get to know students, there may be several students that live in our area that go to the school. I am sure my mom will meet people and their parents and I will find out soon. But so far, it's just Derek.

Chapter 11 - She's Up to Something… I just know it.

For real. Where is Bishop? There is still no sign of Bishop. Unless he is coming in very late at night and leaving very early in the morning with no interaction with anyone at all, I am still convinced that Bishop is in the rose bushes. Unless the Bishop is on some tour of duty in the military or circumnavigating the globe spreading the word, he should have made an appearance at home by now. I see new cars parked by the basement and the lights are on down there. I know they have children, so they could be visiting or she could be hosting foreign exchange students something. I have to keep an eye on what's going on.

If you recall, there are not many kids in the neighborhood. Now that I know Derek lives here, I asked him what was going on and where all the children were. He said he never really thought about it. I found out that they moved into the neighborhood before and had lived here longer than we had. He was also still playing soccer during the off season so he was usually out training, playing, or hanging with his friends from the team. But, since I brought it to his attention, he didn't recall too many kids either.

Derek and I aren't really friends. We only have that one class together and we didn't really make a connection when I attempted to try out for my school's soccer team. He has a brother, who was in my grade, that used to attend the school but he left and I knew him a little better.

He asked me where I stayed and when I told him, he asked if I knew anything of the house next door. I immediately perked up and asked which house? I knew he was probably referring to the Bishop's house, but there is also something weird about the house on the other side as well. *I don't think that I've ever even questioned the house on the other side of us. It is interesting that a church Bishop now lives in that house, or did live there if you count that he is in the rose bushes.*

Derek said he had heard things about that house although until now he had never really given it a second thought. However, since I brought up the issue about not many kids being in the neighborhood, he thought he would share the thoughts he
had. Because kids are always on their computers and rarely come outside these days, it's not unusual for no kids to be out and about. "Strangely, many years ago", he said, "kids were disappearing in the neighborhood". He didn't really have specific children but he had heard that when they went to his neighbor's house. In addition, the children often didn't return. Derek didn't give much credence to the rumor. He just figured that his mom didn't

want him roaming the street so she said things like that to scare him and his brother.

I can't imagine that kids can just go missing and no one is looking for them or it's not on the news. *Maybe it's some sort of religious cult.* I hope they don't invite us over for anything. Now I really have to keep my eyes open. *Has Ms. Rose buried the Bishop and is she kidnapping neighborhood kids too?* This is way too much! I am sure that she is glad Bernard is causing a distraction, but I will have to keep my eyes open.

My brother takes forensic science and says there are chemicals and fertilizers that can mask the smell of a decomposing body. That only makes me think that Ms. Rose is out there making sure there is not a smell that draws any attention.

Sometimes there are animals over there in her yard digging around. We live in a heavily wooded area so we see deer, foxes and sometimes coyote sightings are reported. The HOA encourages people to not leave their small dogs out because the coyotes and foxes might try to grab them. *I never really thought about it but the animals could be trying to unearth something in that yard.* This all seems so farfetched. I am sure Ms. Rose is a nice old lady and that Bishop must come and go in the evening while I am not paying attention. *I am sure there is a rational story behind all of this and I have let my imagination get the best of me.*

Chapter 12 - Facing the Inevitable

My brother has been low key as he prepares to graduate from high school. I am proud of him but I am also a little nervous about him going away to college.

My mind is all over the place with Ms. Rose, Bernard and of course school. All of his college acceptances have started to roll in, scholarships have been offered, and he is just so calm about it.

I know that I've expressed my feelings about him leaving but he's so nonchalant about it. It's just the two of us. We are less than two years apart so we have done everything together.

If he played Tee Ball, then I had to play Tee Ball. When I played soccer, he had to play soccer. When he played basketball, I sat there and watched him play basketball.

When I played volleyball, he sat right there and watched me play volleyball.

My mom was adamant that she wasn't driving all over town to various sports and activities. We were young so we participated in whatever we got registered for.

Since the move and being in high school, we can participate in whatever is of interest; as long as it's not too far away.

Luckily, his top school choices are not too far away and I will be able to see him regularly. He is pretty low profile but I think he is excited and I am proud of him.

What will I do with myself when it gets closer to graduation? We have a pretty small school compared to other schools in the district. I am a part of the school dance ensemble and was able to perform at the graduation last year. My mom asked if I was able to participate this year and I am not sure. That's a few months away so I will see if I get selected to participate.

When he got his acceptance into his first choice college, the admissions staff came to school and it was a big deal about the announcement. I cried and cried so I may need to just sit down with my family on this one. It's still kind of unreal. My mom was very emotional as well so I may need to be there to support her. But, who will support me? I think Aunt Jan will be just as bad as my mom.

We are a very close family. Aunt Jan doesn't have children so me and my brother are like her kids that she can send back to my mom at the end of the day. She has always been around us and participates in everything just like my mom. My brother is the first grandchild and only boy so this is a big deal for the family.

Graduation is a big deal for most families, but for our household it's a huge deal. We are in a family full of high school and college graduates, so we need to make sure he keeps with tradition. I am sure his classmates and their families are going through the same thing.

Furthermore, I hope that we can resolve this missing neighbor issue before my brother leaves because I cannot deal with this situation alone. I just can't.

Aunt Jan gets it but my mom keeps telling me to steer my attention in a different direction; something other than the neighbors' yard. *These television marathons about criminals is not helping the situation at all! They're making me want to prove my theory.*

Suddenly I realize that I will be preparing for college soon as well. I probably need to spend some of the time that I use monitoring the neighbors exploring colleges and preparing for the SAT. *Wow. We can't stop time.*

Chapter 13 - A New Friend

Derek has been great about telling me things about the neighborhood. I told him my suspicions about the neighbor. I thought he would think I was weird and I needed to get a life. He actually said that he had his own suspicions about neighbors in the community.

His mom shared things that she'd heard but of course it all seemed made up. Derek said that the Bishop was not Ms. Rose's her first husband. She had been married before and that the husband got a mysterious illness and died. There were no questions ever raised about it because it all seemed normal and natural. Sickness happens to people so, he was buried and that was it. It was done.

She married the Bishop as soon as her husband died and they have been married ever since. I was in awe as Derek was telling me all about this. I didn't even question where this information was coming from.

He also said that after they moved to the neighborhood, young children started to go missing. It all seems too weird. *Why wouldn't people report missing children? Why wouldn't people turn the whole neighborhood upside down looking for children?* "Well", he said, "the people in the Home Owners Association were leaders of a religious cult".

Many neighbors were involved and that they often met at the Bishop's house. *That would explain why cars are always over there like they are having church or a party or something! I guess there could be some sort of rituals happening over there.*

"You mean that you think she killed her first husband and that they are running a cult and kidnapping children? ", I asked. "Derek that's too much like something you would see on TV!"

I couldn't help but rolling my eyes at the thought of the poor old lady next door being at the center of a cult. I told Derek that seemed too outrageous then, we moved on to happenings at school.

He was trying to determine whether he wanted to go to the prom or if he should go hang out with his friends that night. After other small talk, we got off the phone. Derek is cool. Jace and I are still friends but nothing really happened other than that. We still talk every day at school and I like him but now I think we are just better as friends.

Derek told me about his parents' divorce and how he has to split his time between two different places. He said it's stressful. I can only imagine that having to go to two different places and having different sets of rules could be hard.

I asked him how his brother was handling things, and he said fine.

His brother is so involved in sports that I don't know if he thinks about it. I'm sure it's still hard on him and his parents as well.

When we played T-ball, the parents all seemed so friendly and nice. I was only three at the time so that was 13 years ago.

I only vaguely remember the coaches and parents and if my mom had not said anything to his mother, I would not have made the connection.

Derek is welcome to talk to me about how he feels. I can't change the situation but at least he has someone to talk to about his feelings. He also has to keep me posted on what he learns about the neighbors. I wish my mom would talk in more detail with his mom and see what she meant by be careful. *Are we in danger? Do I need to avoid going outside?*

I do believe something is going on over there. *Where is the Bishop? I wonder if she has him held hostage with the kids in the basement.*

After Derek and I finished talking, I called Aunt Jan to tell her the new information I acquired from an 'outside source'.

I really needed her to help me investigate the situation. *I need closure!* Aunt Jan was all too eager to talk and Google search. I don't really have much information but we can always start with their address.

I also needed to find out if anything happened in our house before we moved in. I have seen shows where people died in the house, and their spirits remained and haunted the house. *Could there be secret compartments in the house and I need to go on a treasure hunt?* We made the purchase from the bank so we never got a chance to meet or speak to the previous owners about the house. I have my work cut out for me.

Chapter 14 - Criminal Minds

After about 250 episodes of Criminal Minds, me and Aunt Jan are ready to investigate this situation. I don't know the Bishop's name and I only know Ms. Rose by…Ms. Rose. That may not even be her real name.

Aunt Jan went online to look up the tax records for their address to get the owner. The property is owned by a company and does not list the names. This is interesting. We think he is a Bishop of the BEC church, so we looked up the church to see who the Bishops were in Atlanta.

We think we at least have a name. The picture we found looks like the Bishop but I haven't seen him in so long, that I am not sure. Maybe if we try to find his wife, it will show a picture of Ms. Rose.

It's been a year since I've seen the Bishop. Aunt Jan found a revival that shows a man that looks like him but it was dated a year ago. We can't find any more recent videos. So, now we are checking social media, websites, and anything else that might show that he is alive. So far we've found nothing. *Hmm. Was he even really a Bishop? What is going on here?* When we look in the Homeowners Association directory, it also just lists the company.

I told Aunt Jan what Derek said about the missing kids and asked her to search for anything that might determine if there were articles about a religious cult or missing kids.

We really don't know who the neighbors are or what is going on. While I'm was on the phone with Aunt Jan, I heard a loud beeping noise. It sounded like a large truck backing up. I went to the window and saw a large moving truck backing into The Rose's driveway. *Are they going on the run? Ms. Rose and Bishop... if that's even their real names.*

"Aunt Jan! They are on the run! There is a large truck in their yard. I think they are moving." Maybe when the police were here for Bernard, they thought it was too close for comfort and they are fleeing town.

I wonder what's in those boxes. They have holes in the sides. That's weird. Who puts holes in moving boxes?

Aunt Jan pulls up as I continue to look out of the window! I heard my mom open the door and say "Jan what are you doing here?"

Aunt Jan asked if she had talked to me recently. Mom said "no, what's going on?"

Immediately, I run downstairs and tell my mom that Ms. Rose and the Bishop are about to go on the run and they are moving the kids that they kidnapped!

"Sierra, I thought you were over this! What is going on?" My mom exclaims. "You

can't just go around saying people are murderers and kidnappers!"
Uh oh! This has gotten out of hand. I ask my mom to let me explain as she side eyes Aunt Jan. My mom says "Jan, have you been playing into this?"
Aunt Jan says "Of course."
"Why are you over here?" My mom asked. Aunt Jan explained the call and said that she thought we might be in danger. "What??" my mom says and stares at both of us like we each had grown a third eye!

I start with the conversation I'd had with Derek and finish with the internet research Aunt Jan and I have been doing. I explained to my mom that when I told Aunt Jan that the moving truck was in their yard, I guess she needed to see for herself.

Mom seemed annoyed. However, me and Aunt Jan decided to stand in the garage and watch what was happening next door!

Ms. Rose looked up but this time she doesn't wave or speak. She focuses on the moving truck and the boxes that are being loaded. *She's picking them up as if whatever is in the boxes is heavy, yet she's being very careful when putting them down.*

My dad drives up and he wonders what we are doing standing in the garage. We tell him that Ms. Rose is packing up and going on the run. Sarcastically, he rolls his eyes, just looks at us and goes in the house.

What have I done? These may just be some old people moving but I still haven't seen the Bishop. Now they are moving things. I haven't seen them bring out any furniture, just the boxes with the holes. While Aunt Jan and I are in the garage pretending to clean out the car and garage, we lose track of time and hear footsteps.

My heart starts beating fast as I notice its Ms. Rose coming up our driveway. What do we do? *Does she know that I'm on to her? Is she coming to kidnap me?* Well, that will not happen. Aunt Jan and Mom wouldn't let that happen…*but what does she want?*

Ms. Rose says hello and makes small talk with Aunt Jan. Again, she seems to think that she is my mom. She says they are moving a few things and will be gone for a while and she didn't want us to be alarmed when other people were at the house. She left a number in case *she* needed to be reached. She still did not include her full name nor did she mention the Bishop.

I called Derek to tell him what happened today.

"Be careful Sierra. I know this started as a joke but you may be on to something."

I think Derek is aware of more than he is telling me.

"Aunt Jan, should we look up this phone number?"

Unfortunately, when you google the phone number it doesn't give you any information. We were in the very same place we were before! Not sure of their names, who they are, where they are going or what is the happening in that house. *Where is the Bishop and what is buried under those bushes?*

As I head into the house, my mom starts telling me about activities she wants to sign me up for in the city. I know she is trying to refocus my attention but I am in enough stuff and I don't think I need to sign up for anything else. She isn't trying to sign my brother up for anything. Probably because he is busy applying for scholarships, waiting on acceptance letters and trying to figure out where he is going to school.

I really think I am trying to keep myself occupied so that I do not have to think about my brother going to college.

Chapter 15 - Bernard Is Going Down

It's been very quiet at Bernard's house. He hasn't been on the news since his press conference declaring his innocence. I haven't seen any news trucks lately so perhaps the investigation is just working its way through the system. Sometimes I will see a few toys in the yard but I haven't seen his wife or any cars. The most activity in the yard has been the mail truck leaving things in the mailbox. The blinds have been down but those Christmas lights are still in the bushes and the *"Yard of the Month"* sign is still on the lawn.

The reports indicate that there are several people tied to this case so it should be interesting when they get to the bottom of things. He seems like a nice person but you never really know people. The charges that they mentioned on the news were pretty bad and several people that work with him have plead guilty to a variety of crimes. I don't know exactly was it all means but I wouldn't want to be in his situation.

It looks like a car is pulling into his driveway. He and his family have probably moved somewhere else to avoid the media coming over to ask questions. *They can be very aggressive with people.* When you watch the news you can see that the reporters just walk up to people start bombarding them with questions.

That person doesn't look familiar. They appear to be walking around the house and looking around. Maybe they are just checking on the house to make sure that no one has tried to break into it; just in case his family comes home. I hope he isn't guilty of the various charges that have been outlined. I watch a lot of law shows and if he gets a good and creative lawyer, he may be able to beat the charges. He is a lawyer as well so maybe that will help his situation.

Just as I suspected, here comes Bernard and there is a little head poking up in the back of the car. I guess they needed to come back home to get something. The little girl bounds out of the car and runs through the yard. I bet she misses being at home and able to run in her yard. Maybe this is their routine and I just never noticed what was happening at their house.

One of the people in his office has to go to jail for almost two years. I am sure that person will tell everything she knows so that she can get a reduced sentence and get back home.

I can't imagine having my face plastered all over the television for illegal things. This should be a lesson to all. Think about the possible consequences to determine if it's worth it. *Wait. He is coming out of the house. Who is that in the car? I can't tell if it's his wife or someone else but it is a lady with lots of hair.* I wonder why she didn't get out of the car.

I decided to go downstairs and see what my mom thinks. I know that she is going to ask if they are taking down the Christmas lights.

"Mom, I think Bernard is at the house." I said.

She looks at me and shakes her head. "Sierra, you have such a vivid imagination", she says.

"Are they by any chance taking down the Christmas Lights?" I knew that question was coming! It is somewhat of a joke for us now. I laugh as I look back to the window and notice that they are pulling off and the Christmas lights are still intact.

The next evening on the news they showed Bernard back in court to respond to some additional charges. *I told you that his staff person was going to talk.* She probably told the investigator things they didn't even ask for. *Save yourself at this point.* I hope the little girl is okay. She is pretty young and probably doesn't understand what's happening. *Just keep her away from Ms. Rose's house.*

Chapter 16 - That Only Helped for a Little While

My mom signed me up the extra activities anyway. They have kept me pretty busy but they have also kept her busy. She has to drive me and my brother to different places.

School is going well and I have also signed up for activities there as well. I am finally getting into a rhythm. I met a few people that seem cool and maybe we will become friends. We will see how that works out.

I haven't seen Derek in a while at school. I hope everything is okay. I know his brother left the school and it's not like him to miss class. I will have to ask his friend Chad where he is and hope that he doesn't start anything with me.

The computer class is really self-paced and the teacher doesn't do a lot of interaction with us. Most of the lessons are online and he just provides guidance as we work on our projects. We have headphones in so there is not a lot of interaction in the classroom among students so I don't really know Chad well. I just know that he and Derek play sports together and perhaps he knows where he has been. I'll ask at the end of class.

"Hey Chad, have you seen Derek?" I asked.

"No, I haven't seen him this week. He hasn't been at practice so maybe he is sick or something." Chad responded. Chad went on to tell me that he sent him a text and he had not responded and that that wasn't like him. The coach said he had not heard from him or his mom either.

"Okay, Thanks." I said. *I wonder what's going on with Derek.* I didn't think much of it at the time but I hope he isn't sick. His brother isn't here anymore so I can't ask him. I don't remember whether or not my mom got their phone number at home because he didn't respond to my text either. Maybe he got in trouble and his mom took his phone. *That's a stretch but maybe.*

When my mom picked me up from school. I gave her the rundown from the day. There were some interesting things happening at the school and so much to keep up with. There was nothing super exciting just a lot going on. The middle school kids seemed to just run everywhere and they are so rude. My mom keeps reminding me that I was probably like that in middle school and the older kids probably said the same thing about me. *Ugh! I hate it when she does that...makes it seem like I'm being irrational!*

As we pulled into the neighborhood, I saw Derek's mom parked in front of our house. "What is she doing here." My mom asked me.

“I don’t know.” I responded. “Derek hasn’t been at school for the past few days so I hope everything is okay.”

My mom rolls down the window before turning in and says “Hi, are you waiting for me?” Derek’s mom responds yes and she looks upset. My mom pulls into the driveway and gets out to go talk to her and see what’s going on. I wave, head towards the house and go in. I wonder what’s going on.

I head straight for the window to see if I can tell what the two moms are saying. Derek’s mom is pointing towards Ms. Rose’s house as they talk intensely. My mom looks confused and then looks toward the house as if she knows I’m watching. *I am watching*. And, I am about to call Aunt Jan is give her the details. Details of what, I don’t know yet, but she will understand.

"Aunt Jan, guess what?" I say. I share with her my day and what led up to mom in the yard talking. She asked if his mom looks sad, angry or like she just needed to talk. I tell Aunt Jan that I didn't think of them as friends but maybe she had some questions about school or maybe the neighbor. As I continue to watch them, my mom gives Derek's mom a hug and then heads toward the house. Derek's mom gets in the car but doesn't drive off immediately…of course, I am waiting anxiously by the door to see what's going on… and Aunt Jan is on the phone waiting as well.

"Mom, what's going on?" I asked.

"I'm not sure exactly." Mom responded. "Let me get my things out of the car, I'll be right back."

When mom steps out of the door, we hear a crash. I run outside and see that a car has crashed into the neighbor's fence! My mom runs out to see if everyone is okay and tells me to call 911.

Derek's mom is still outside. She gets out of her car as well. In the wrecked car, the airbag has deployed and there is blood everywhere. *Oh my gosh! This is scary!* I tell Aunt Jan I will call her back and I dial 911.

I tell my mom that the paramedics and police are on the way. I've never seen this car before but I hope the person is okay. The police and paramedics arrive. They are blocking our driveway trying to render aid. I called Aunt Jan back and asked her to get my brother from practice because we will not be able to get out of the driveway with the police, fire department and paramedics on the scene.

My mom stands back and watches *when this happened!* Derek's mom said that the car was driving so fast that as she was pulling off it almost hit her. Then, when it tried to avoid her, the driver lost control and slammed into the fence. It looks like the person will be okay but the fence has had it. *I wonder if this is a time to call Ms. Rose?*

After things settle down, the police got the information and asked about the owners of the house. My mom explained that they were out of town but she had a number if that helped. Mom came in the house to get the phone number for the police officer.

A few moments later, Aunt Jan and my brother pulled up. The tow truck was still blocking our driveway so they had to park at the neighbor's house and walk over. By this time, a few other neighbors had gathered.

I continued to wait patiently…well, not really patiently… for my mom to tell me what she talked about with Derek's mom. *I just have to know!*

Chapter 17 - Who Is that Kid in the Yard?

The next morning, I went outside to put my things in the car. I have to be at school late today so I will have to go straight to practice. I looked next door and there was a kid walking around, then there were more. I was stunned and stopped to watch them. they looked disoriented and the downstairs door was open. The kids wave at me and I hesitantly wave back. Suddenly, I see another kids waving at the ones in the yard. They appear to be telling them to come back inside. The first child I saw looks afraid. I shake my head and hope that I am dreaming. I walk back into the house and tell my mom what I saw.

"Mom! You will not believe what I just saw!" I exclaimed. "There was a kid roaming around at Ms. Rose's house. Then, other kids were in the basement telling him to come back in."

There is definitely something weird going on over there. Before we could pull out of the driveway, Ms. Rose pulled up and looked like she wanted to assess the damage to her fence. She said hi and asked if mom had a time to talk.

Mom said no, because I needed to be at school early. My mom said she would call her a little later. To which Ms. Rose replied, "please do".

We don't usually go out this early in the morning. *I wonder if those kids are Ms. Rose's kids or if she is really hiding kids in the basement.* I hadn't seen anyone over there since Ms. Rose left in the large truck. Maybe the kids needed help. I still haven't heard from Derek.

My mom said that his mom, just wanted to get her feedback about the school because she was considering withdrawing Derek. My mom, in turn, told her that we were too new to the school to really give an assessment. She informed her that we hadn't had any issues. My brother was about to graduate and he was doing pretty well.

There was so much going on the other day that I couldn't get a full story from my mom. Essentially, Derek had to leave to go with his dad for something out of town and they had limited access to the phones or internet. It was sort of retreat in the mountains that lasted for a couple of weeks. *Perhaps that's why Derek wasn't responding to me or Chad. Maybe the coach knew where Derek was but didn't want to share it with the other students.*

This all seems so weird. I think I just need to focus on school and my activities. This is a lot for a teenager to keep up with. I called Aunt Jan just to chat and she immediately asked for my mom.

I gave my mom the phone because Aunt Jan seemed upset. My mom took the phone but didn't say a word. She was listening intensely and then she got up and walked outside.

What was that all about? I turned on the television and started watching one of the ID channel shows called the Neighbor Next Door. I looked out of the window and my mom was just standing there just listening and looking confused. *What's going on out there?*

A few moments later, Aunt Jan pulled up and got out of her car. She looked concerned so I didn't bother her or my mother. She pulls out her tablet and starts showing things to my mom. They both look alarmed, confused and keep looking back because they know I am probably watching them.

My mom shook her head intensely. I tried to focus on the TV but that wasn't really working. The show was about a neighbor who seems like a nice old lady but she was really kidnapping kids. *Just what I need. Another show to freak me out about the neighbor.*

As I am looking out the window. I see a little hand waving from Ms. Rose's basement window. It's one of the children from this morning. *How can she see me? Does she need help? Is she trying to get my attention?* I stepped away to get some water and when I return, she was gone. My mom is still looking at the tablet with Aunt Jan. *I think my mind is playing tricks on me.*

My mom and Aunt Jan finally come in the house because the tablet needs to be charged.

"Hey Auntie!" I say.

"Hey Sierra, how as your day?" she asked.

"It was okay, what's going on?" I inquire.

"I'm not sure. Let me finish talking to your mom and then we can talk, okay?"

They went to the other room as my mom continues to look at whatever is on it. Next, I hear my mom ask, "What do we do?" *Do about what?* I wonder.

Chapter 18 - I Am Speechless

My mom asked me to come into the room and I am nervous. *What is this all about?* She looks like she is trying to gather her thoughts. Aunt Jan may have found the Bishop. I gasp and ask "What's going on?"

Aunt Jan had been doing some research and investigating since you told her that you thought Ms. Rose had buried him under the bushes. She was able to find out about the owners and occupants of the house. This led to her finding out some interesting things.

Based on her findings, Aunt Jan said, the Bishop went on a mission trip out of the country. Aunt Jan was able to find a blog that highlighted the journey with pictures and prayer groups and circles. She was able to get information about Ms. Rose and the things that she is involved in and some background information about the neighborhood. As Aunt Jan talked about her revelations and shows me the information I am in awe. I have invested all of this time in Bishop being in the bushes and he is on some remote island in Tristan da Cunha*? I feel let down!*

We all talk a little about the situation and laugh. I think about all of the time I invested and just like that…mystery solved. While we are chatting I tell them about the child I saw in the driveway the other day and share that she was waving from the window while they were talking. I fear that I've let my imagination get the best of me. Then, I share that I haven't seen my friend Derek in a while and really wanted to let him know what we learned. *I guess I'll have to wait until his dad brings him back.*

As my mom is browsing the blog, she says it's odd that there are no pictures on here. The videos that are posted are old videos and were made before Sierra noticed that he was missing. At least we had a name for the Bishop and Ms. Rose. We hadn't seen him in so long, I asked my mom to let me see the videos and the blog. As I am browsing, I laugh and note that yes that's Bishop.

While Aunt Jan and my mom pour a glass of wine, I get to a picture in the blog. I read the post for the day and caption. I tap my mom on the shoulder and slide the tablet back in front of her.

"Mom, that's not the Bishop." I shared.

She spits her wine out and says "What?"

I repeat, "That's not the Bishop."

I looked at my Aunt Jan and just shook my head. My mom says it's been a while since we had actually seen him.

"No Mom", I said, "that's not him. If he is on a remote island somewhere they are not likely to have internet access to post a blog."

As I keep scrolling through the posts, I looked at the people standing in the background. There was a person behind the man in the picture that looked familiar. I couldn't place him but he was familiar.

As my mom and Aunt Jan continue to talk. I continue scrolling and looking at the info Aunt Jan brought. Suddenly, I yell out. "That's Derek!"

My mom is startled and asks "Your friend Derek?" *This is insane!*

Then the doorbell rings. We all look at each other wondering who could be at the door. We sit still hoping, they go away. My mom says, "Okay, calm down, It's probably a package delivery." She goes to get her phone to look at the front camera.

It was a package delivery. We all breathe a sigh of relief.

Everyone tries to regroup. I am still wondering why Derek is in that picture. The man looked familiar because he is Derek's dad, our T-Ball Coach when I was three. *What is he doing in Tristan da Cunha?* That is one of the most remote islands in the world. *Are there even people there*?

My mom begins to share the conversation she had the Derek's mom. She said that Derek was scheduled for a weekend with his dad. He was only to have a short vacation but they didn't come back as scheduled. She has been working with the police to see what her options are because she hasn't been able to contact her ex-husband or Derek to get an understanding of what was happening.

Derek had missed school and she thought they may be in danger. The Bishop had been working with Derek's dad as his spiritual leader and they would often go to remote places for spiritual cleansing.

It was okay in the beginning but then he would come home speaking irrationally. Derek's mom thought he was being brainwashed. Now she believes that Derek was taken to one of these spiritual retreats and that Derek will get brainwashed like the other kids.

I was quietly listening because I was speechless!
Other kids? What other kids?

My mom went on to tell me that Derek's mom thought that the Bishop and Ms. Rose were running a spiritual cult where they were brainwashing kids in the community. They pretended to host church services in their home for parents who were having difficulty with their children's behavior.

This explains why there are no kids in the neighborhood walking around. I couldn't imagine that kids were missing and no one was reporting this to the police. They are being brainwashed and taken to this remote island for spiritual cleansing. The large truck moving the boxes with holes in them were probably kids being transported out of the house. *Now it makes sense.*

But, who is the young girl that was waving from the basement?

Chapter 19 - I Need to Get to The Bottom of This

As I sit back and reflect on everything that has happened, I am still in awe. This is a lot to consume. *How will we get Derek back home? What's happening with the girl in the basement? Is she scheduled to go with the next batch of kids? I know she is probably not supposed to be outside. She looked scared and the little boy that was calling her back also looked scared.*

As we continue to talk the doorbell rings again. This time it's the little girl from basement. *How did she get out of the fence? What do we do?*

We all go to the door and my mom opens it. The little girl looks confused and says she is hungry. My mom says okay and asks where her parents are, she says she doesn't know. She proceeds to ask if she can also have food for her brother.

“Where is your brother?” my mom asks. The little girl asks for water.

I think we should call the police, but my mom is just asking the little girl questions. “Are there other kids in the house? Where is Mrs. Rose?” my mom asked.

The little girl says that someone usually comes over to bring them food but no one has been back to the house since the car accident at the fence.

I forgot about that, the car damaged the fence and it has not been repaired just yet. That’s how she got out and over to our yard. The little girl stares at me. My mom asked her name and she says, “Bailey”. Her brother’s name is Noah.

My mom asked where her parents were or if Ms. Rose was her grandmother. My mom said she had her number and could call, but the little girl said “No, please don’t call her. I am not supposed to come out of the house but I was hungry. I saw the pretty girl and she seemed nice and I thought she could help me". My mom looked at her sister and told her to call Terrance. Terrance is our cousin who works for the Police Department. He would come over and tell us what to do.

"Bailey would you like your brother to come over and get some food?" my mom asked. She said no, she would take him something if we allowed. As my mom was preparing something for Noah, I heard my Aunt Jan talking to Terrance. Terrance is a detective so he wasn't in a police uniform.

We introduced Bailey to Terrance and gave him the information we had about the whole situation. It was unbelievable but Bailey was strong enough to get back up and go over to get Noah.

Within moments there were several police cars on the street. We stepped into the garage to see what was happening. Terrance had asked Bailey how many other children were in the basement. She said right now it was just 4 of them. The other kids were taken away to go get healed. She seemed so smart and well spoken. She was small but she said she was twelve years old and her brother was nine years old. The other kids were eight and six. I guess with Bailey being the oldest, she was taking care of the group. When they ran out of food she came outside hoping to find help.

Within moments the officers had three young kids walking out of the basement. Terrance asked if we had any contact information for the homeowners. I shared the phone number Ms. Rose left. We were outside with the kids and the police officers to see if the kids wanted to come in and eat something while they waited on social services.

Bailey was very talkative. The other children just sat quietly and ate. Terrance didn't ask many questions. He said the social service worker needed to be present before her could ask any questions. But, Bailey wanted to chat so I talked her as Terrance and the other officers listened.

After about an hour the social services worker rang the doorbell. I am sure my mom was not expecting to have this activity happening in our house, but they needed a place where the social services worker could speak to the children, get their information and make plans for their care until they investigate what was happening. Terrance called the number we gave him, Ms. Rose answered the phone. He told her there was an incident at the home and he needed her to come if she was able.

By this time the officers had a search warrant and were making preparation to go into the house.

Ms. Rose pulled up just as Terrance and the other officers headed up her driveway. When the gate opened, the officers showed her the warrant and proceeded to enter her house. Ms. Rose looked distraught as neighbors started to gather.

My mom called Derek's mom and suggested she come over and perhaps shed light on what was happening. She came over quickly and immediately shared what she knew and what was happening with her son.

We don't know how many kids are involved, when this all started or where the parents are for Bailey and Noah. The other kids belong to another family. *How could all of this be happening right next door*?

I knew something weird as going on next door but I didn't actually think they were really kidnapping children. When I looked up, they were escorting Ms. Rose to the police car and the kids were getting into the car with the social service worker.

I wonder where the Bishop is and if he will come back to help her. That would be hard to do from under the rose bushes.

While my cousin Terrence was here I told him of my suspicions. Very quickly the K-9 unit pulled up and the dogs were out on the property searching the yard. We heard a loud howl. My cousin stood up and walked out the garage. He got on the phone and I heard him say, “Max hit on something. I need you to bring the forensics team”. From watching all of the crime shows, I knew exactly what that meant. I knew that meant that they found something…something interesting!

My brother had been in his room the entire time, working on his project. He found enough time to come down stairs and see Terrance outside on the phone, K-9s sniffing the property, and Ms. Rose in the back of the police car. All he had to say was, “Got em.”

Chapter 20 - Sierra, Wake Up.

It had been a long day. I can't believe that all of this happened in the neighborhood. I am so tired; I think I will lay down for a nap. That was too much excitement for one day. While I was asleep, I felt someone shaking me.

"Sierra, wake up. Sierra, wake up." My mom said.

"I just went to sleep mom, can I have a few more minutes?" I ask.

"No, you have been asleep all day, it's time to get up. Sierra you need to shower and unpack." She says.

I am tired. All of the things that happened yesterday have me exhausted and I may need a few days of sleep. I sit up and ask if I can just have a few more moments to sleep. So much went on yesterday and the preceding days that I needed some rest.

My mom asked, "What went on yesterday that has you so tired?"
I looked at the clock then looked at my mom. I asked her what happened to Ms. Rose and where did they take Bailey and Noah?

She looked confused and asked, "Who are Bailey and Noah? I don't know them but you have been asleep for the past 9 hours. I know you are tired from the move but you need to wake up, and get something to eat."

I looked around the room and there are boxes everywhere, I go downstairs and Aunt Jan is unpacking boxes and trying to help set up the kitchen.

My brother is listening to music and eating and yells "Glad you could join us Sierra. We have been unpacking boxes all day while you slept."

It's not possible. *Was I dreaming?* I walked outside and there were boxes everywhere. Here comes a kid speeding down the street on his bike. I looked next door and there is an older lady watering the bushes. She waved as her garage door opened. Out walked a man with a tray of flowers. He places them next to the lady in the yard. They have shovels and soil laid out ready to work in their yard.

I stood there watching so the gentleman walked over to the fence and says, "You must be Sierra, we met everyone else but they said you were tired from the move and were asleep. Welcome to the neighborhood."

Standing there looking at him, I was unable to speak. The man sensed that something was wrong and asked if I was okay. I snapped out of it and said, "Hi. Yes. I am Sierra."

He says, "I am Bishop Johnson and this is my wife, Rose. I know you must be tired from the move. Once you and the family get settled, we will have to invite you over."

My mom stepped out with more boxes and walked over to the fence. "I see you met Sierra, she says. "She has been asleep all day. It has been a lot to get moved and situated so we are all tired."

Bishop Johnson responded, "Yes, we understand so, we won't keep you. Again, welcome and we hope to have you all over soon. Take care and God bless you and your new home."

Thank you.

This is all so weird. I can't believe this was all a dream. I head back into the house to get something to eat. Everyone else is buzzing around the house and unpacking. I sit down and try to eat but I can't stop thinking about Bailey and Noah.

I finish up and head upstairs where I attempt to start unpacking and sorting my clothes. I can't help but look out of the window. My mom comes by the room and sees me staring out of the window and asked if I needed some help and if everything was okay. I said yes, but she sensed something else. She came into the room to talk to me about change.

I let her talk but I kept an eye on the window. She said she knows moving was hard for me. She knows that I hated leaving all of my old friends behind and going to a new school. She assured me that things will be great at the new school. She says I'll make new friends in the neighborhood and we are closer to Aunt Jan and grandma. I just said okay and continued to stare out the window.

She kissed me on the forehead and then headed down the hall to check on my brother's progress. I turned and followed her. My brother had unpacked everything, organized his closets, put everything in his dresser drawers and made a pile of things to give away; things he no longer wanted.

Was I really asleep that long? He is laying on his bed listening to music and singing along. My room has boxes stacked to the ceiling. I should have listened to my mom when she said to get rid of things when we were packing. Now I have all of this stuff to go through and I don't need or want half of it! This will take me forever to unpack.

I miss my friends. I needed to talk to someone about my dream or nightmare… It was so vivid, everything about it seemed real and I can't get the thought out of my head.

I turned on my music and got into a groove unpacking my boxes. I have so much stuff to go through, I may ask Aunt Jan to help. She can make quick decisions about what I need to keep and what I should donate. After all, I will be going to a new school and it requires a uniform. I am not excited about having to wear a uniform. Everyone dressed exactly the same seems weird. But maybe it will be easier getting ready in the morning.

I finally get most of my things unpacked and get my bed made. Since I slept all day, I am not sleepy. The cable and internet have not been connected yet so I can't watch television. I don't want to disturb anyone else and I am almost afraid to go back to sleep. Finally, I doze off and here comes my brother telling me to get up and come get breakfast. Although I am tired, I get up so I can get my body back on track since we have to start preparing for school.

Everyone is up and chipper at breakfast. We still have boxes everywhere but it's coming together and the house is starting to take shape. The breakfast discussion turns to me and my mom asked how my unpacking was going and if I needed any help today. I told her that I was good. Aunt Jan helped me unpack and the other boxes will just have to wait. It's just knick knacks that will probably get donated. My mom said I seemed distracted and that something was bothering me. I still couldn't believe it was all a dream and I am hesitant about telling anyone about my dream. It was so crazy but it seemed so real. What really stunned me is that the neighbor's house was in my dream, the neighbor is a Bishop and his wife is Mrs. Rose. I think tonight, I will talk to my mom. Maybe she can help me make sense of it all.

The stress of this move has me freaking out. My mom came by my room to check on me and I told her I had a weird dream the other day and it has stressed me out. She could tell I was really bothered so she sat on the bed and prepared to listen. So, I shared with her all the things that happened in my dream from the Bishop going missing, Mrs. Rose burying him in the rose bushes, the coach kidnapping his kid and taking him to a remote island and Ms. Rose kidnapping and holding children hostage in her basement. She just listened. When I say it out loud, I realize that it sounds crazy and must have been a dream. My mom hugged me and said, "Sierra, the move has been stressful, and you are tired. All of that seems a little weird but we watch a lot of the crime shows and maybe it just all came together in your dream."

Maybe she is right. Let me try to get some sleep because I will have to go looking for uniforms and my mom has scheduled a visit to the school ahead of the open house event. She wants us to see everything before it is filled with parents and students so that we can have some familiarity with the school and my brother and I can focus on meeting new people and teachers.

The next morning, we get up and head to the school. Some of the people are familiar because my mom works in the area so it's new as a school but we come to the area all the time. There are a few other people at the school. It sounds like they are transferring students and are making sure their enrollment papers are in place before the Open House. I meet a few students and at least I will know a few people before we come to the school.

Chapter 21 - Open House

This has all been a world wind. It's time for open house and as we are leaving, I glance over to the neighbor's house. I see Ms. Rose in her yard planting roses. I can tell she takes pride in her yard and spends a good bit of time tending her flower beds. They will be beautiful when they are in full bloom. As we drive through the neighborhood, I see plenty of beautiful lawns and rose bushes. Kids are riding their bikes down the street and neighbors are chatting. I think we will be okay. And although I miss my old neighborhood friends, I hope to make some new ones.

As we turn into the school, there are plenty of people there this time and I am nervous. My brother is acting like it's just another day. He says we know some of the kids that attend the school from the YMCA, so it will be fine. He is so calm but I am a nervous wreck. Here we go.

When we walk into the school, I hear someone scream, "Sierra!" I turn around and its Laila. "What are you doing here?" I asked. She said that she was coming here for high school. Laila and I met at a dance camp when we were in middle school. She was cool and we had a great summer but we lost contact during the school year. I am so glad to see her. She said a few of the other girls were there as well. This is a relief! At least I will know a few people.

I left the area with Laila to find the other girls. It was so good to see them. We all went to different schools and made a connection at the dance camp. We aged out of the program so we haven't seen each other in a while. We would see each other periodically at the Atlanta Ballet or for supplemental activities the dance program offered throughout the year.

As we went from room to room meeting teachers and administrators, I see a few people from the YMCA. I think we are all glad to see familiar faces. My brother is over there mingling with people he knows from playing golf and some of the leadership programs he attended so he will adjust just fine.

My mom is off chatting and hugging people. She called me over a few times to introduce me to parents she knew and I met their students. I felt better knowing a few people at the school. I even walked into one of the rooms and saw a teacher who attends my church. She gave me a hug and told me she is right down the hall so if I needed anything she was there. She took me to meet some of the other teachers and told them I was one of her kids and to make sure I was taken care of. I smiled and said thank you. *This may work out after all.* We have a stack of paperwork to sign and review and class assignments that we must have ready when we return to school. This will put us a little ahead when we come to school on the first day. We have a long list of supplies to purchase as well. I know the stores will be crowded, luckily we start before all of the other schools so maybe we can get ahead of the crowd.

As we prepare to leave and head to the parking lot, mom spotted someone she says looks familiar. We walk that way and when the lady turns around, she smiles. My mom says, "you look familiar. Are you Sherry Jones?" She said "Yes. You look familiar, too."

My mom says, "I'm Jasmine from the 3-T Dodgers, our kids were on the same team! Is that Derek?"

In many communities, the rose symbolizes balance. The beauty of this flower expresses promise, hope, and new beginnings. It is contrasted by thorns symbolizing defense, loss, and thoughtlessness. In literature a rose often symbolizes love and beauty. As I journey through life, I know that I need to have balance. I think about all of the things the kids do in school and activities they may participate in outside of school. These things can be stressful and at times challenging.

I am inspired by hope and the opportunity for a new beginning. Everything that a rose symbolizes is relative to life. The thorns represent things that we will go through; experiences that may not always be positive. Those experiences teach us things that are necessary to navigate through our lives. Most of us have been pricked at least one time and have learned that we must handle the rose gently to avoid the thorns.

New beginnings can be very stressful but with the support of family and friends, it can also be an awesome experience. I learned very valuable lessons.

Be open about going new places and learning new things. Fear can paralyze us and keep us from experiencing life to the fullest. I encourage people to try new things and be open to exploration.

Communicate your needs. Many times, I think we expect our parents to just know what we are going through. We have to communicate when we are scared, nervous, or have some concerns.

Give people a chance. In school, many kids feel judged based on their looks or where they live. You have to give people a chance to show who they are. You may miss out on great friends if we don't give people a chance.

Plant roses.

Made in the USA
Columbia, SC
09 May 2019